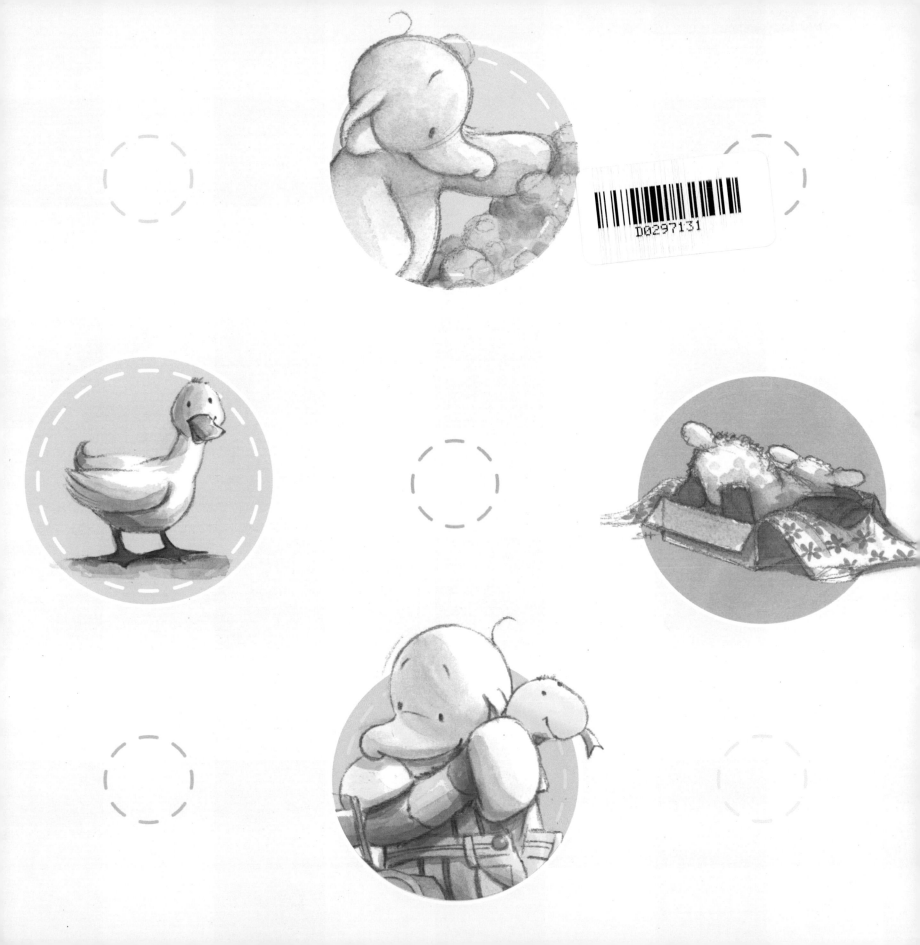

Humphrey's Treasury

Sally Hunter

igloo

This edition published in 2011
by Igloo Books Ltd
Cottage Farm
Sywell
NN6 0BJ
www.igloo-books.com

www.humphreys-corner.com

B044 0711

2 4 6 8 10 9 7 5 3 1
ISBN: 978-0-85734-712-1

Printed and manufactured in China

Humphrey's Treasury

Sally Hunter

igloo

This igloo book belongs to

Contents

6

Humphrey's Farm Adventure

It was a lovely, sunny day and Mummy had taken Humphrey and his little friend, Tilly, to the farm on Duffy's Hill.

Humphrey wanted to go and see the animals straight away, but Mum said, "Let's have our picnic first."

Humphrey was too excited
to finish all his lunch.
He kept his apple for later.

Mum bought some animal
feed and filled up Humphrey
and Tilly's buckets. "Let's go!"
shouted Humphrey.

First of all, Humphrey and Tilly said hello to the sheep.

They were very pleased to see them, especially with the treats!

Humphrey liked the baby lamb the best.

The ducks made a lot of quacking noise when they saw Humphrey.

Humphrey said they must like him very much, because they followed him down the path.

Humphrey and Tilly thought
the pigs were very cute!

There were five little
piglets, too. They had floppy,
pink ears and curly tails.

Tilly wanted really badly
to take one home.

The cows were nice and friendly
and seemed very interested
in Humphrey and Tilly.

"I think they like our snacks
more than the grass!" said Tilly.

Humphrey made friends with the
smallest one. He called him Moo.

Next, Humphrey said hello to the chickens. They made clucking noises and wanted to see what was in his bucket!

Oh! There is a VERY cheeky one!
She found Humphrey's treats and
decided to finish them up!

Oh, dear! That's all the
snacks gone and Humphrey
and Tilly still needed to
visit Henry the Horse.

What a good job Humphrey
still had his apple. Henry had
the nicest treat of all!

Tilly stroked Henry
on his soft nose.

Humphrey and Tilly have said
hello to all the animals.

Mum made them wash
their hands two times.

Then they were allowed to choose
a farm book each, from the gift shop.

Humphrey and Tilly have had
a wonderful day at the farm.

Goodbye, Tilly.

Goodbye, Humphrey.
See you soon!

Humphrey's Playtime

Humphrey doesn't go to school yet,
so he has lots of time to play.

... the train, blocks, boat, Octopus, Caterpillar... and all the other toys.

Other days, Humphrey plays with his special painted animals.

"All aboard!" he says.
"We are going on an adventure!
Come on, Pinky, up you go."

And sometimes Humphrey paints a lovely picture for Mum. She especially likes rainbows and smiley sunshine faces.

"Da da da daaaa...
I'm a Superhero!"
shouts Humphrey.

He runs around the
house, jumps off
the chairs and makes
a lot of noise!

"Have you finished saving the world yet?" asks Mum.

Humphrey likes playing dress-up in big shoes!

He walks about in them. Clomp, clomp!

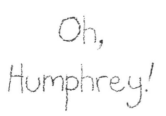

Dad was late for work because his best shoes were in the toy box.

Oh, Humphrey!

Henry Horse takes Humphrey on long journeys to different lands. It is very exciting!

But they have to be back in time for tea.

One time, Humphrey got lost at sea...
there were lots of monsters!
Good Job Mop came to help.

37

Driving his little red car up and down the hall
is one of Humphrey's best games...

... but sometimes he bumps into Mum's legs.
Oops, Humphrey! Be careful!

"Oh, dear!" says Humphrey. "Sounds like there is a problem. Don't worry, I will fix it...

... and then it's time for a good wash!"

39

Humphrey has lots of fun in the garden, too. He has a look for George, who lives next door.

Then makes
roads for his cars
and trucks...

... and builds
little houses out
of stones for
the fairies.

In the garden,
Humphrey
has his very
own swing.

"Hello, Miss Birdy. How are you today?" he asks.

42

Humphrey has some creepy crawly friends, too.

"Come on, Simon, Sally and Sam Snail," he says. "Off we go! Choo, choo!"

Dad gets Humphrey's bike out
of the garage. "Look, Dad!
Soon I can go on a big boy's bike!"

"Come on, Mop, we are going for a ride. Hold on tight!"

Humphrey has lots of lovely days, playing in all these different ways...

But most of all,
Humphrey likes...

... looking after...

... cuddling...

47

... playing with...

... and loving, Mop – his soft,
floppy, one-eared little rabbit.   x

Goodbye, Humphrey.
See you soon!

Humphrey's Jungle Adventure

Humphrey's little friend George, who lived next door, had come over to play for the afternoon.

Humphrey was excited to show him his new, big, jungle adventure book!

Humphrey fetched his really good lion mask, too –
"Look, George, I made him at nursery."

Then George had a
really good idea.
"Humphrey! Let's have our
very own jungle adventure."

"Back in a minute!"
shouted George.
He disappeared through
the hole in the hedge,
into his garden.

"Hmmm,"
thought Humphrey,
"Mum's plant pots
could be very
useful."

"Look, Humphrey," said George, "I've brought Stripey."

George had his best toy in his arms — a soft, floppy tiger, with a purr in his tummy.

"Good idea, George," said Humphrey.
"I found these for our jungle, too."

Next, Humphrey asked
Baby Jack nicely, if he could
please borrow Cheeky Monkey.

"Thank you, Baby Jack,
I will bring him back soon."

Then, Humphrey looked for Polly Parrot. Where had she gone?

George helped, too.

"Oh, there you are!" said Humphrey. Polly had been sitting in the treehouse.

Humphrey asked Lottie if
Bear was allowed to come
and play Jungles, too.

Lottie said, "He was about
to have his tea, but okay then.
Make sure you look
after him well!"

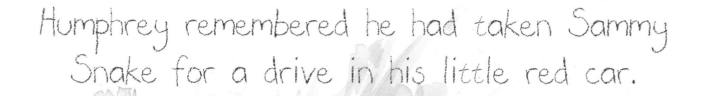
Humphrey remembered he had taken Sammy Snake for a drive in his little red car.

"Come on," he said. "Come and be in our jungle!"

"Hurray! We have lots
of animals now."

Suddenly, Humphrey and
George heard a BIG noise!
A loud, growly kind of noise –
G-R-R-R!

A big, furry lion had come
into Humphrey and
George's Jungle!

Phew! It was
just a friendly
Daddy lion.

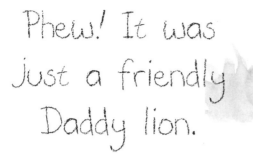

Humphrey and George each had a lion ride.

Then they had pineapple juice and chocolate animal biscuits in their tropical jungle.

Goodbye, George!
See you soon, Humphrey!

Humphrey's
Bedtime

It was Baby Jack's bedtime.
Humphrey and Lottie tucked him in.
"Night, night, sleep tight," they said.

Baby Jack had to go first because he was the smallest.
Next, it was Humphrey's bedtime.

Lottie said, "I am allowed to stay up very, very late. That's because I'm the biggest."

Humphrey got his toys
ready for bath time.

He made big bubble
mountains...

... and magic potions.
Humphrey had a lovely time.

Lottie still wasn't getting ready for bed.
She said her babies needed a really good wash!

"PJ's on, Humphrey," Mum said.

Humphrey had hot milk and buttery toast.

He felt warm and cozy in his tummy.

Mop liked his, too.

But Lottie didn't have time for supper.
She said, "Oh, no... it's my babies' tea time.
Eat it all up and you will grow big and strong."

Humphrey had a horsey ride!

"Neigh! Neigh! Up the wooden hill to bed."

Humphrey had fun seeing how high he could fly.
Mum said, "I think it's story time, now!"

It was Humphrey's special book.

"Once upon a time, a little pixie lived at the bottom of the garden," said Mummy. Humphrey was all snuggly ... and sleepy.

Humphrey didn't hear how the pixie
and his friends lived happily ever after
because he fell asleep before the end.

Ssssh... goodnight, little Humphrey. x

Lottie still wasn't getting ready for bed!
She was having problems with her babies.
Lulu was being silly.

Trevor wouldn't get ready for bed properly.

Barry wouldn't lie down...

... and Bear had got lost.

Lottie felt all hot...

... and CROSS!

Daddy came in from work. "What's all this?" he asked. "Come on, my funny little girl."

"Off we go," he said.

"To bed."

Goodnight, Baby Jack,
Humphrey and Lottie.
Sweet dreams. x